LEXINGTON PUBLIC LIBRARY   9891

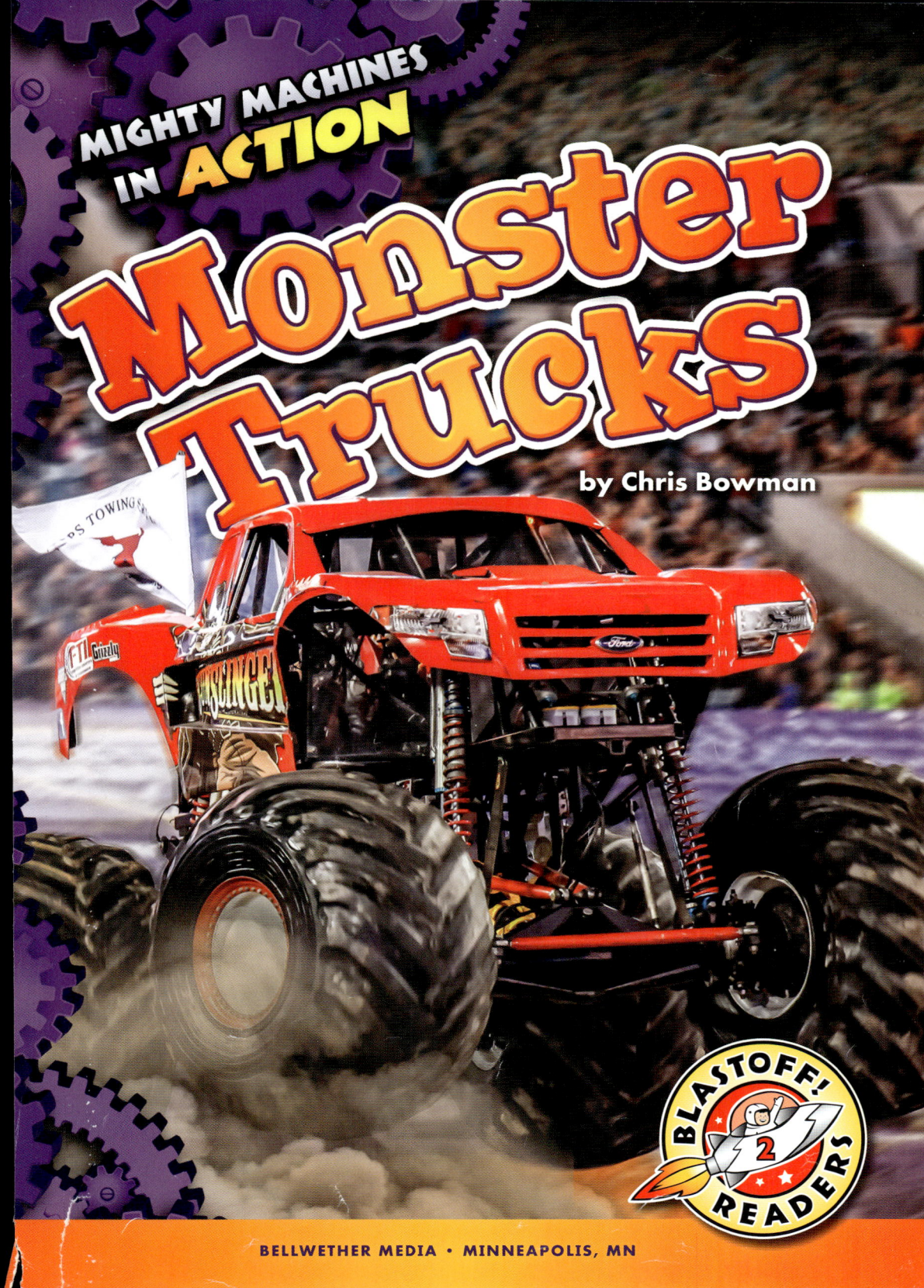

Note to Librarians, Teachers, and Parents:

Blastoff! Readers are carefully developed by literacy experts and combine standards-based content with developmentally appropriate text.

Level 1 provides the most support through repetition of high-frequency words, light text, predictable sentence patterns, and strong visual support.

Level 2 offers early readers a bit more challenge through varied simple sentences, increased text load, and less repetition of high-frequency words.

Level 3 advances early-fluent readers toward fluency through increased text and concept load, less reliance on visuals, longer sentences, and more literary language.

Level 4 builds reading stamina by providing more text per page, increased use of punctuation, greater variation in sentence patterns, and increasingly challenging vocabulary.

Level 5 encourages children to move from "learning to read" to "reading to learn" by providing even more text, varied writing styles, and less familiar topics.

Whichever book is right for your reader, Blastoff! Readers are the perfect books to build confidence and encourage a love of reading that will last a lifetime!

This edition first published in 2017 by Bellwether Media, Inc.

No part of this publication may be reproduced in whole or in part without written permission of the publisher. For information regarding permission, write to Bellwether Media, Inc., Attention: Permissions Department, 5357 Penn Avenue South, Minneapolis, MN 55419.

Library of Congress Cataloging-in-Publication Data

Names: Bowman, Chris, 1990- author.
Title: Monster Trucks / by Chris Bowman.
Description: Minneapolis, MN : Bellwether Media, Inc., 2017. | Series: Blastoff! Readers: Mighty Machines in Action | Includes bibliographical references and index.
Identifiers: LCCN 2016033335 (print) | LCCN 2016034284 (ebook) | ISBN 9781626176065 (hardcover : alk. paper) | ISBN 9781681033365 (ebook)
Subjects: LCSH: Monster trucks–Juvenile literature.
Classification: LCC TL230.5.M58 B69 2017 (print) | LCC TL230.5.M58 (ebook) | DDC 629.224–dc23
LC record available at https://lccn.loc.gov/2016033335

Text copyright © 2017 by Bellwether Media, Inc. BLASTOFF! READERS and associated logos are trademarks and/or registered trademarks of Bellwether Media, Inc. SCHOLASTIC, CHILDREN'S PRESS, and associated logos are trademarks and/or registered trademarks of Scholastic Inc.

Editor: Christina Leighton   Designer: Steve Porter

Printed in the United States of America, North Mankato, MN.

Table of Contents

A Monster Show	4
Racing and Tricks	8
Bodies, Engines, and Shocks	12
Flying High	20
Glossary	22
To Learn More	23
Index	24

A MONSTER SHOW

Cheers fill the **arena**. Fans are excited for the monster truck show.

The trucks **rev** their engines. Then they take off!

One truck hits a jump. It flies through the air.

Then it drives over a row of cars. Nothing can stop this machine!

RACING AND TRICKS

arena

Monster trucks need a lot of space!

Shows usually take place at arenas or fairgrounds. Fans fill the **bleachers**.

Sometimes, the trucks race. They speed around tight turns and over jumps.

MACHINE PROFILE
GRAVE DIGGER

First model built: 1982

Power: 1,500 horsepower (1,119 kilowatts)

Monster Jam World Finals Racing Champion: 2004, 2006, 2010, 2016

In **freestyle** events, they do tricks. They spin, crush cars, and soar through the air.

BODIES, ENGINES, AND SHOCKS

Monster truck bodies are made of **fiberglass**. The bodies all look different.

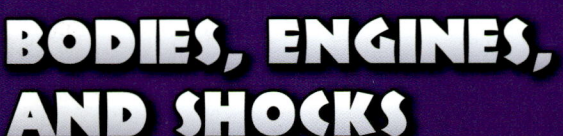

fiberglass

The trucks are painted and given names.

Monster trucks have loud **supercharged engines**. These power the trucks into the air.

shocks

Shocks allow the trucks to hit jumps at high speeds.

Huge tires help the trucks **grip** the course. They are more than 5 feet (1.5 meters) tall!

Metal **roll cages** protect the drivers during crashes.

Most drivers sit in the middle of the truck. A **harness** keeps them in place.

A switch near the driver turns off the truck. A remote can also shut it off.

IDENTIFY A MONSTER TRUCK

- painted body
- huge tires
- shocks

FLYING HIGH

People come from all over to watch monster truck shows.

The trucks amaze with their power and tricks. They continue to draw big crowds!

Glossary

arena—a big area surrounded by seats often used for sports, music, or other events

bleachers—rows of seats for many people

fiberglass—a strong, lightweight material made of plastic and glass

freestyle—a monster truck event in which the trucks do tricks

grip—to tightly hold

harness—a set of straps that keeps the driver safe

rev—to turn a part of the engine; the engine makes a noise when it revs.

roll cages—steel frames inside trucks that keep drivers safe if the truck rolls over

shocks—the parts of monster trucks connected to the wheels that soften the feeling of jumps and crashes

supercharged engines—powerful engines that burn a lot of fuel

To Learn More

AT THE LIBRARY

Dinmont, Kerry. *Monster Trucks on the Go.*
Minneapolis, Minn.: Lerner Publications, 2016.

Head, Honor. *My Little Book of Big Trucks.*
New York, N.Y.: Scholastic, Inc., 2014.

Silverman, Buffy. *How Do Monster Trucks Work?*
Minneapolis, Minn.: Lerner Publications, 2016.

ON THE WEB

Learning more about monster trucks is as easy as 1, 2, 3.

1. Go to www.factsurfer.com.

2. Enter "monster trucks" into the search box.

3. Click the "Surf" button and you will see a list of related web sites.

With factsurfer.com, finding more information is just a click away.

Index

air, 6, 11, 14
arena, 4, 8, 9
bleachers, 9
bodies, 12, 19
cheers, 4
course, 16
crashes, 17
drivers, 17, 18, 19
engines, 5, 14
fairgrounds, 9
fans, 4, 9
fiberglass, 12
freestyle events, 11
grip, 16
harness, 18
jump, 6, 10, 15
names, 13
power, 10, 14, 21
race, 10

remote, 19
rev, 5
roll cages, 17, 18
shocks, 15, 19
show, 4, 9, 20
size, 9, 16
speed, 10, 15
switch, 19
tires, 16, 19
tricks, 11, 21
turns, 10

The images in this book are reproduced through the courtesy of: Rob Bixby/ Flickr, front cover; Michael Doolittle/ Alamy, pp. 4, 18-19; Natursports, pp. 4-5, 10, 12-13, 13, 15; ZUMA Press, Inc./ Alamy, pp. 6-7; Michele Oenbrink/ Alamy, pp. 8-9; kontur-vid, p. 9 (truck); Michael Stokes, pp. 10-11; Barry Salmons, p. 14; picturesbyrob/ Alamy, p. 16; AP Images, p. 17; Gunter Nezhoda, p. 19; martin berry/ Alamy, pp. 20-21.